Aunty Bexda's Mermaid Tails
Meet Little Bexda!

by Aunty Bexda

♡ Bexda! ⭐

Sweet Little Bexc

Her town was so pre

was born in the fall.

y, and she was so small

Her mommy is Pa
Sweet Little Bexdo

Patches works hard taking care of the sick. If you need a good nurse, she'd be your first pick!

Billy's a rock
He's got lots of

tar who plays the guitar!

ns from here, near and far!

Nana and Inky lived
Sweet Little Bexda t

ight'cross the street!
ught that was so neat!

Cute Little Bexda
Nana Made Bexda
They loved to wa
she also loved to

nd Nana did stuff.
larshmallow fluff!
ch Price is Right,
pend the night!

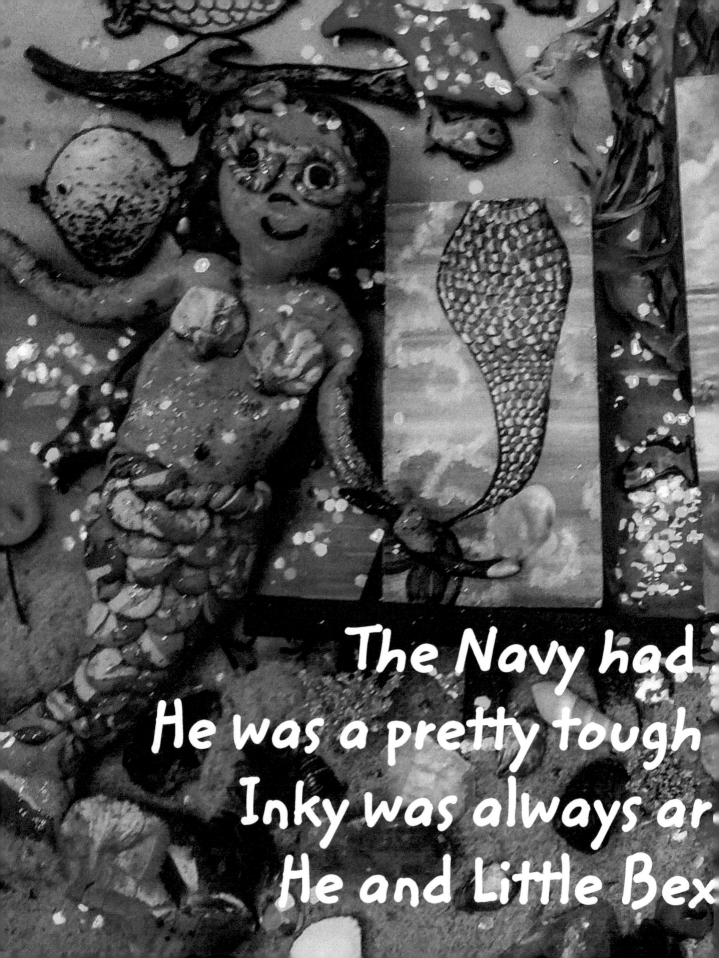

The Navy had
He was a pretty tough
Inky was always ar
He and Little Bex

...ky for 27 years.
...y who had zero fears!
...nd from the start!
... loved to do art!

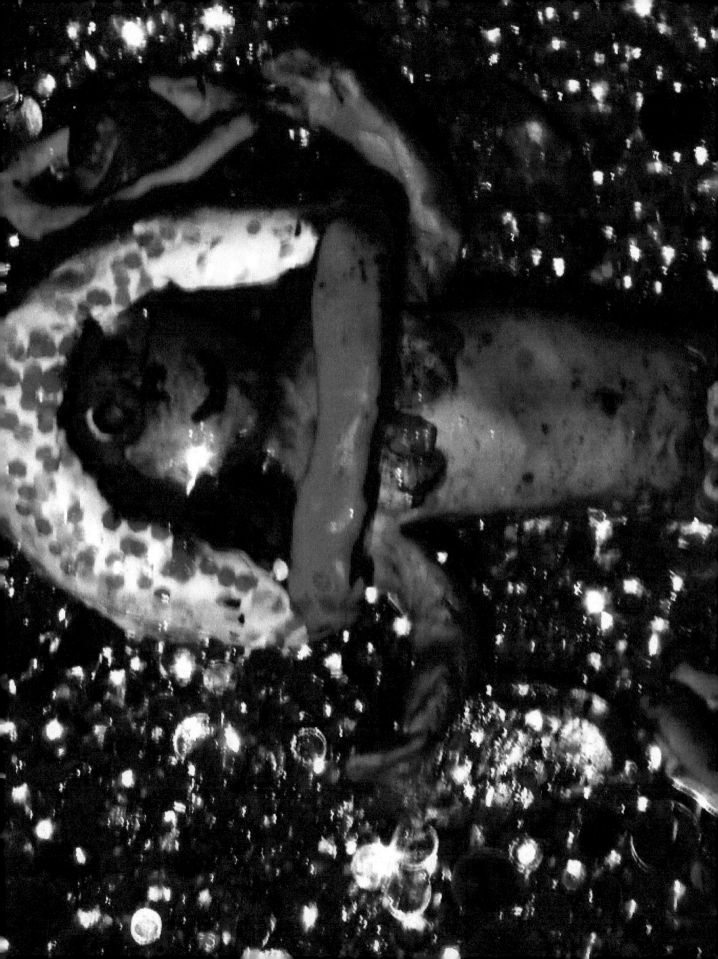

Little Bexdas right eye,
was seriously crossed,
her doctor called it lazy,
but she called it lost!

Gigantic glasses sat on her face,
her eyes looked huge,
...like was she from space!

But she needed those glasses
so that she could see,
plus they looked cute,
and that's always key!

Fun Little Bex.
She played with many
She played with her
There really wasn't m

loved to play!
ngs on any given day!
s, she rode her bike.
h that she didn't like!

Poor Little Bexda
the funny thing is,
Maybe that's wh
inside of a book, h

s super duper shy,
e didn't know why.
e loved to read,
shyness was freed!

She loved to color, she did it so well, and when she was drawing she came out've her shell!

"You're good at art!"
other kids would say...

"It runs in my blood from Jay and Grandpa Jay!"

When Bexda grew up,
she stopped being shy.
As a matter of fact,
this might make you cry
(...laughing!)

got wicked loud and so very funny,
ot tattoos, that cost lots of money!
ose is pierced, and so are her ears...
yes all those things will cause tears!!

She's all of the kids most favorite
they always have a blast and jokingly

She teaches the kids all kinds of art
they smile and they paint...
...but that's only the start!

Aunty Bexda always has a story to tell,
so she's putting them in books,
and it'll be swell!

All of the stories are about her and her friends.
"Aunty Bexda's Mermaid Tails"
is a series that truly never ends!

Dedicated to...
My Mom. My Dad. My Nana. My Inky.

I love you so much.

Shout Outs...
Ruthy. Mr. Rogers. Freddy Mercury. Biggie. Jay-Z.
Cookie Monster. Michaels Middletown, RI staff
(especially Savannah, Scott and Emma). Staples Middletown, RI
staff (especially Elizabeth and Meagan).
Barnes & Noble Middletown, RI. The Carpenters
(my favorite family). Dr. Gendreau.
Dr. Johnsen-Smith. Briana. Roxy. Steph. Jen. Gretchen. Rebecca
Ali. Holly. Olivia. Sofia. Ava. Anthony. Peyton. Paige.
Kingston. Cole. AB. Graham.
You all are the best part of my life.

Thank you.

CPSIA information can be obtained
at www.ICGtesting.com
Printed in the USA
BVHW020555151118
533179BV00002B/1/P